Copyright © 2023 by Bobbi Jarrin
All rights reserved.
No part of this book may be used or reproduced without the author's written permission.

Contact the author at bbbjarrin@gmail.com
Illustrations and cover by Jerri Lott
This book was printed in the United States of America.

 This Blue Bunny

 book belongs to

 _____

A beautiful blue bunny,

with eyes the color of the sky

was sent here on a mission,

but no one knew just why.

He certainly was different,

and maybe some would stare,

he liked what he saw there.

that he wasn't like the rest?

and strived to do his best.

His mama always taught him

that we come in many colors.

if we're not like all the others.

So please be kind,
do good things,

and help out when you can.

a blue bunny for a friend.

Printed in the USA
CPSIA information can be obtained
at www.ICGtesting.com
LVHW070027291023
762448LV00014B/706